Le Renard et la Grue
- une fable d'Aesop
The Fox and the Crane
- An Aesop's Fable
retold by Dawn Casey
illustrated by Jago
French translation by Annie Arnold

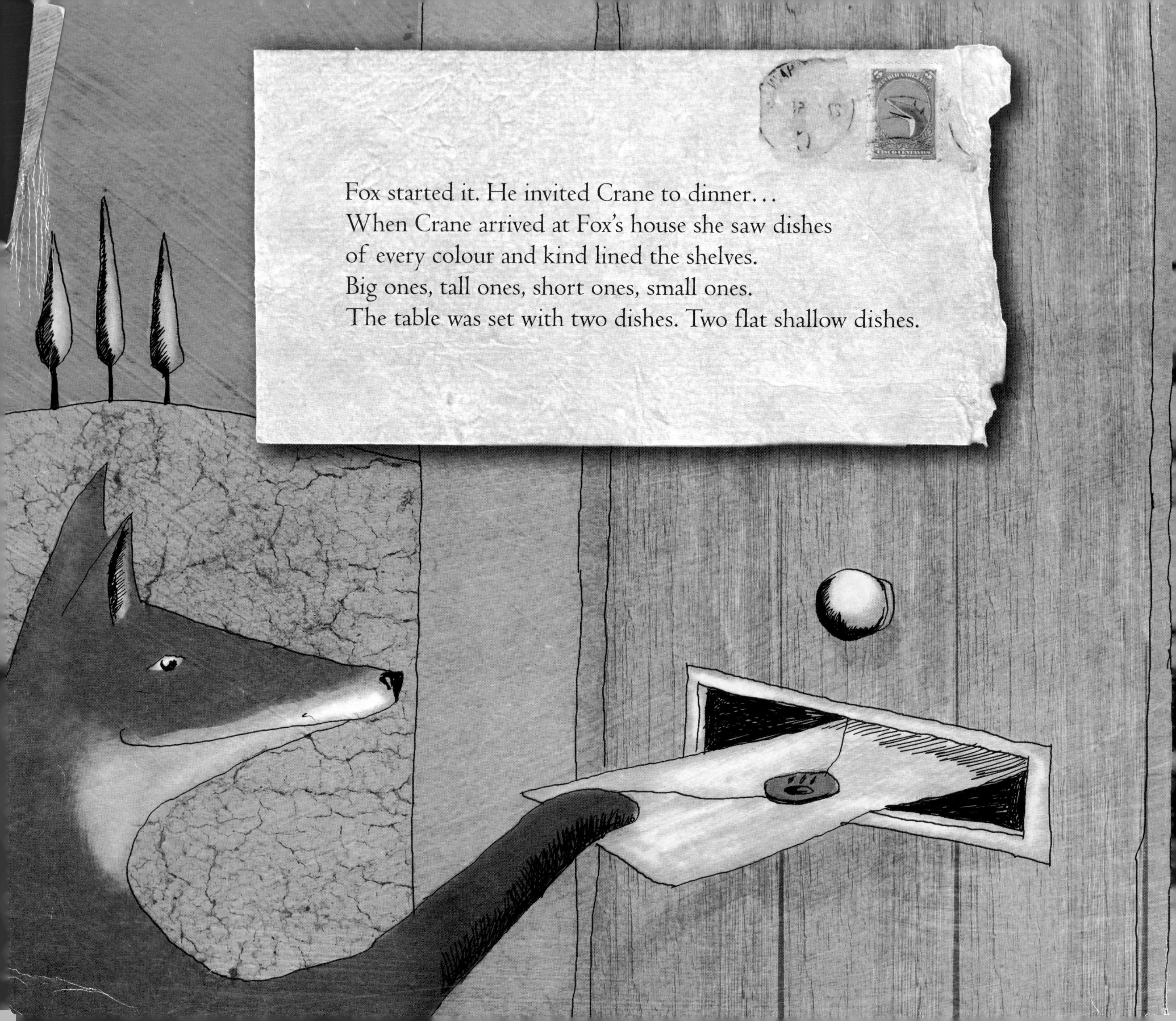

Fox started it. He invited Crane to dinner…
When Crane arrived at Fox's house she saw dishes
of every colour and kind lined the shelves.
Big ones, tall ones, short ones, small ones.
The table was set with two dishes. Two flat shallow dishes.

Le Renard commença. Il invita la Grue à dîner…
Quand la Grue arriva chez le Renard, elle vit des plats de toutes couleurs et sortes alignés sur les étagères. Des grands, des hauts, des courts, des petits.
La table était mise avec deux plats. Deux plats peu profonds et plats.

La Grue becqueta et elle picota avec son long bec fin. Mais peu importe de quelles manières elle essaya, elle ne put même pas attraper une gorgée de soupe.

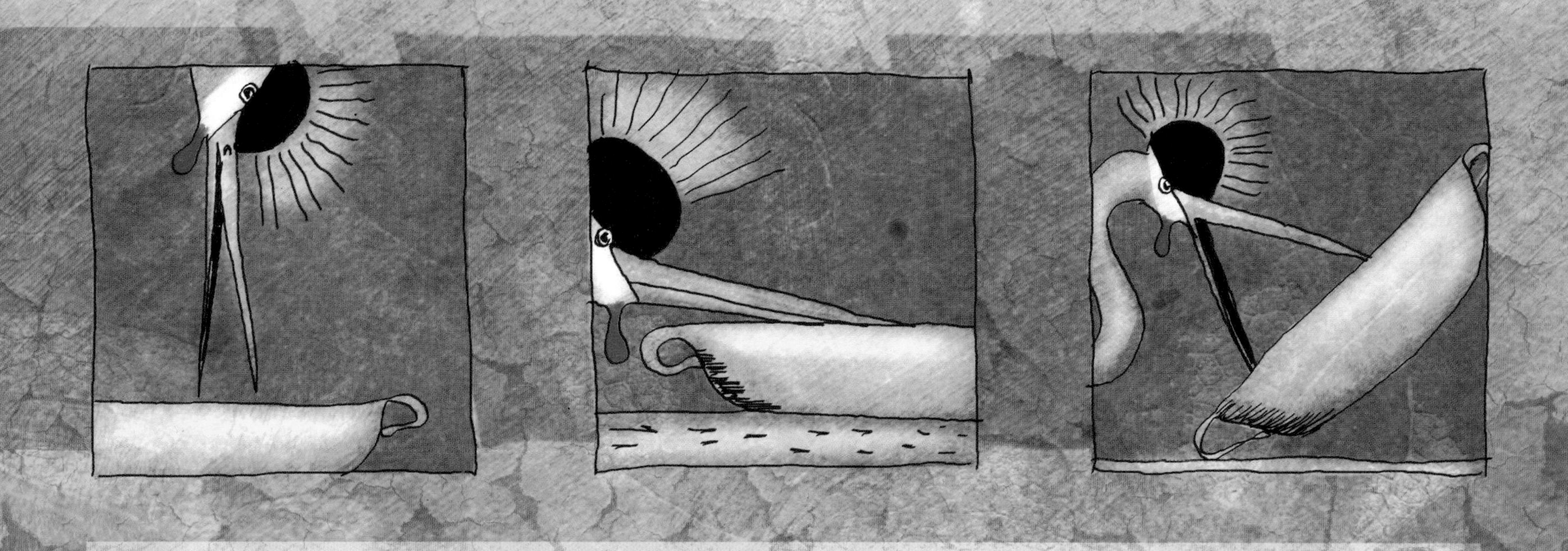

Crane pecked and she picked with her long thin beak. But no matter how hard she tried she could not get even a sip of the soup.

Le Renard regarda la Grue se débattre et ricana. Il souleva sa soupe à ses lèvres, et avec un GLIP, GLUP, GLOUP, il la lapa.
« Humm, délicieux ! » il se moqua, essuyant ses moustaches avec le revers de sa patte.
« Oh, la Grue, tu n'as pas touché à ta soupe, » dit le Renard avec un sourire affecté. « Je suis désolé que tu ne l'aies pas aimée, » il ajouta, essayant de ne pas renifler en riant.

Fox watched Crane struggling and sniggered. He lifted his own soup to his lips, and with a SIP, SLOP, SLURP he lapped it all up.
"Ahhhh, delicious!" he scoffed, wiping his whiskers with the back of his paw.
"Oh Crane, you haven't touched your soup," said Fox with a smirk. "I AM sorry you didn't like it," he added, trying not to snort with laughter.

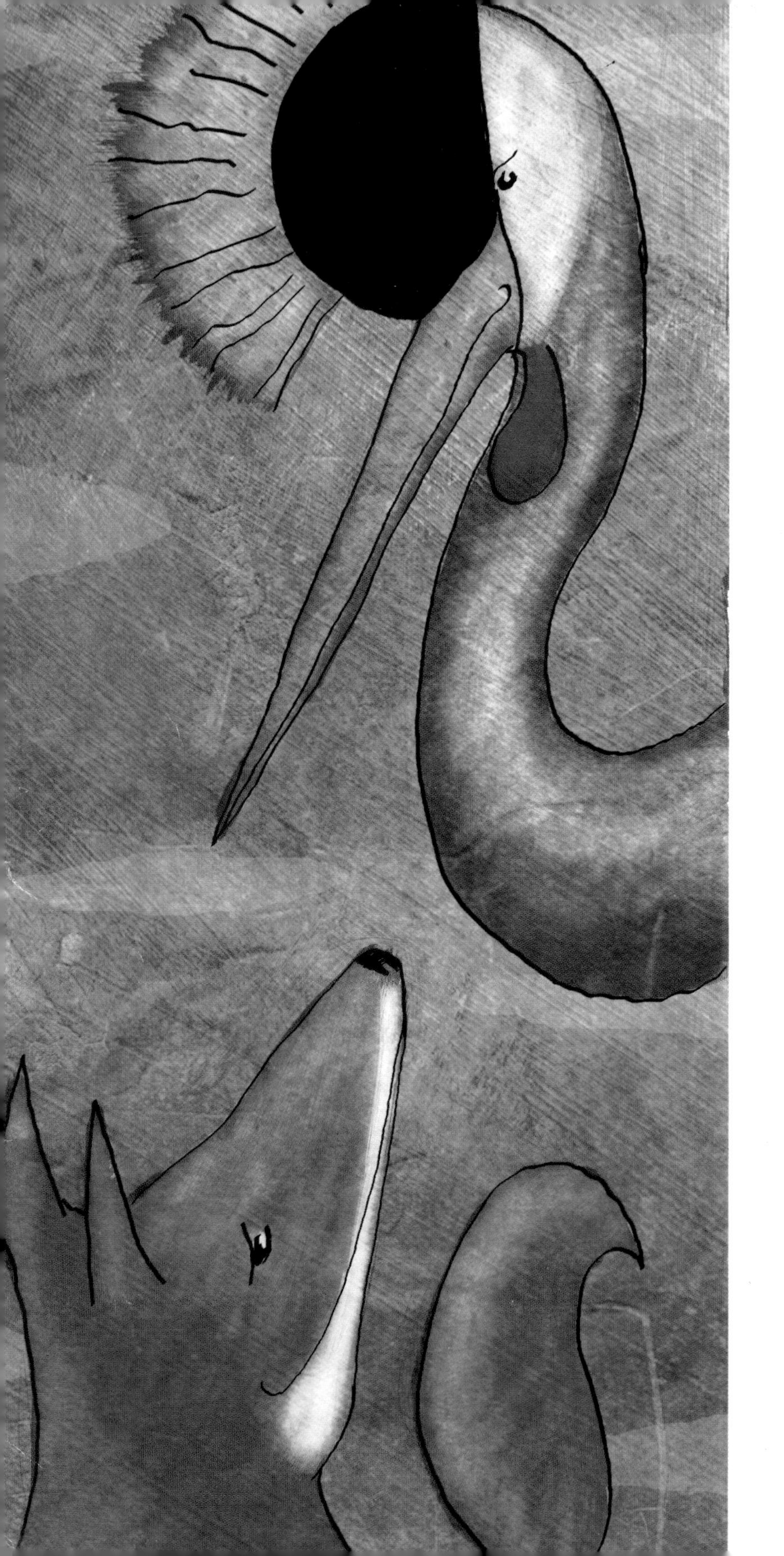

La Grue ne dit rien. Elle regarda le repas. Elle regarda le plat. Elle regarda le Renard, et sourit. « Cher Renard, merci pour ta gentillesse, » dit la Grue poliment. « S'il te plaît laisse-moi te payer de retour – viens dîner chez moi. »

Quand le Renard arriva la fenêtre était ouverte. Une odeur délicieuse s'en échappait. Le Renard souleva son museau et renifla. Sa bouche saliva. Son estomac gargouilla. Il lécha ses lèvres.

Crane said nothing. She looked at the meal. She looked at the dish. She looked at Fox, and smiled.
"Dear Fox, thank you for your kindness," said Crane politely. "Please let me repay you – come to dinner at my house."

When Fox arrived the window was open. A delicious smell drifted out. Fox lifted his snout and sniffed. His mouth watered. His stomach rumbled. He licked his lips.

« Mon cher Renard, entre, » dit la Grue,
étalant son aile gracieusement.
Le Renard passa devant elle. Il vit des
plats de toutes couleurs et sortes alignés
sur les étagères. Des rouges, des bleus,
des vieux, des neufs.
La table était mise avec deux plats.
Deux plats hauts, étroits.

"My dear Fox, do come in," said Crane,
extending her wing graciously.
Fox pushed past. He saw dishes of
every colour and kind lined the shelves.
Red ones, blue ones, old ones, new ones.
The table was set with two dishes.
Two tall narrow dishes.

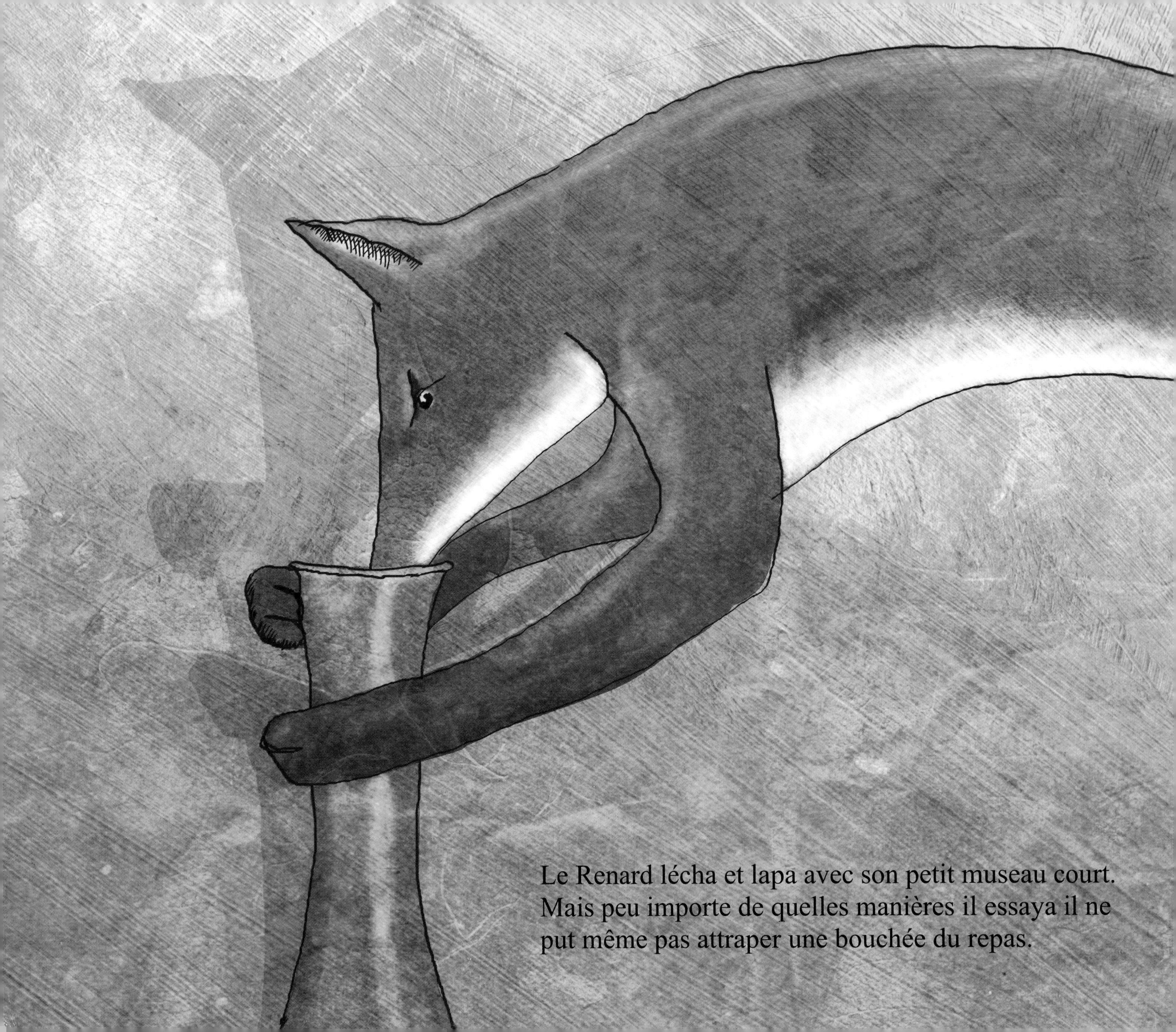

Le Renard lécha et lapa avec son petit museau court.
Mais peu importe de quelles manières il essaya il ne
put même pas attraper une bouchée du repas.

Fox licked and he lapped with his short little snout.
But no matter how hard he tried he could not
get even a mouthful of the meal.

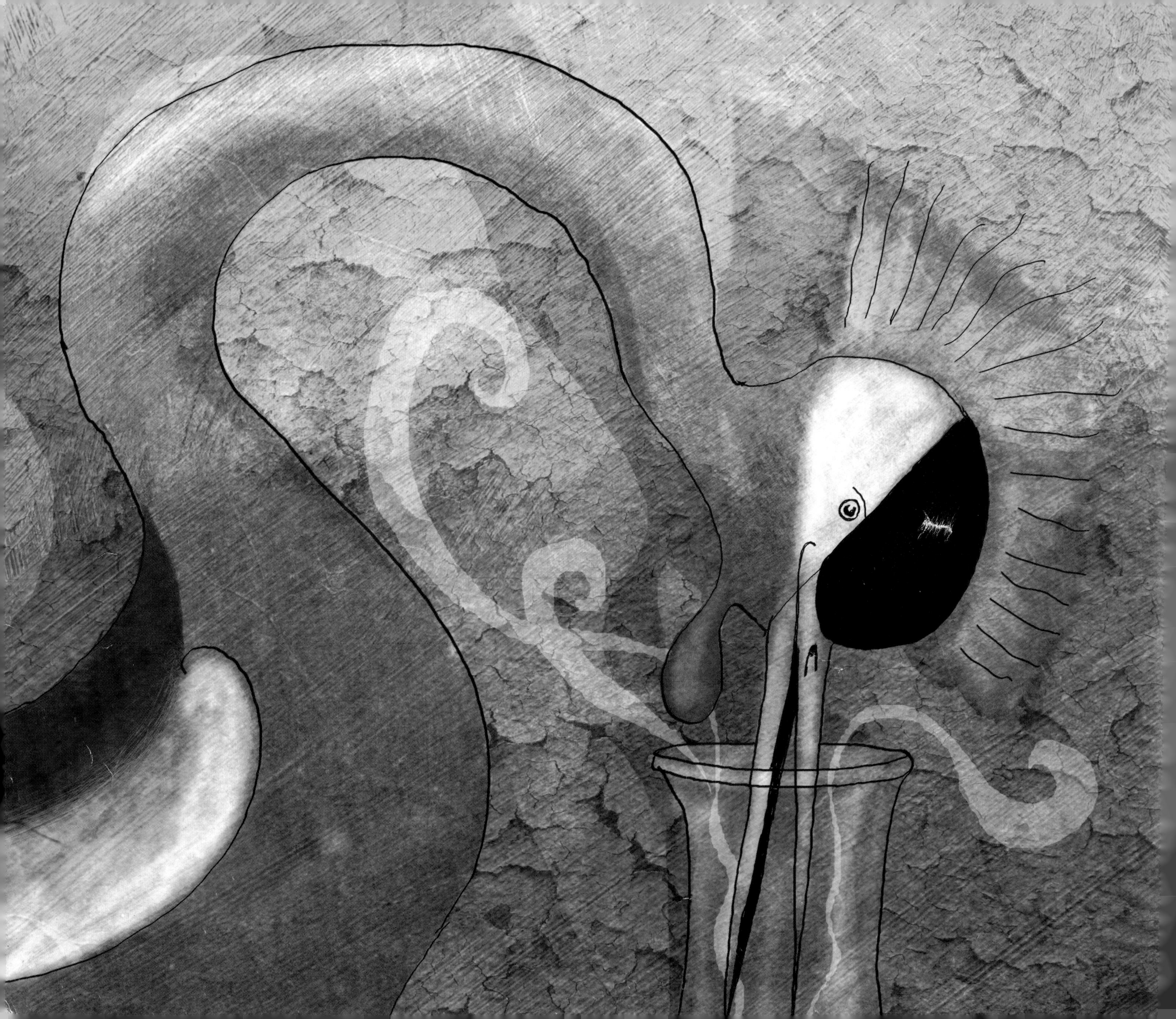

La Grue mangea son repas très doucement, savourant chaque bouchée.
« Cher Renard, merci beaucoup d'être venu, » sourit-elle, « cela a été un plaisir de rendre la pareille. »

L'estomac du Renard gargouillait et grondait.
Et quand il est rentré chez lui, il avait toujours faim.

Crane ate her meal very slowly, savouring every mouthful.
"Dear Fox, thank you so much for coming," she smiled, "it has been a pleasure to repay your kindness."

Fox's tummy gurgled and grumbled.
And when he went home, he was still hungry.

The Fox and the Crane

Writing Activity:
Read the story. Explain that we can write our own fable by changing the characters.

Discuss the different animals you could use, bearing in mind what different kinds of dishes they would need! For example, instead of the fox and the crane you could have a tiny mouse and a tall giraffe.

Write an example together as a class, then give the children the opportunity to write their own. Children who need support could be provided with a writing frame.

Art Activity:
Dishes of every colour and kind! Create them from clay, salt dough, play dough… Make them, paint them, decorate them…

Maths Activity:
Provide a variety of vessels: bowls, jugs, vases, mugs… Children can use these to investigate capacity:

Compare the containers and order them from smallest to largest.

Estimate the capacity of each container.

Young children can use non-standard measures e.g. 'about 3 beakers full'.

Check estimates by filling the container with coloured liquid ('soup') or dry lentils.

Older children can use standard measures such as a litre jug, and measure using litres and millilitres. How near were the estimates?

Label each vessel with its capacity.

The King of the Forest

Writing Activity:
Children can write their own fables by changing the setting of this story. Think about what kinds of animals you would find in a different setting. For example how about 'The King of the Arctic' starring an arctic fox and a polar bear!

Storytelling Activity:
Draw a long path down a roll of paper showing the route Fox took through the forest. The children can add their own details, drawing in the various scenes and re-telling the story orally with model animals.

If you are feeling ambitious you could chalk the path onto the playground so that children can act out the story using appropriate noises and movements! (They could even make masks to wear, decorated with feathers, woollen fur, sequin scales etc.)

Music Activity:
Children choose a forest animal. Then select an instrument that will make a sound that matches the way their animal looks and moves. Encourage children to think about musical features such as volume, pitch and rhythm. For example a loud, low, plodding rhythm played on a drum could represent an elephant.

Children perform their animal sounds. Can the class guess the animal?

Children can play their pieces in groups, to create a forest soundscape.

Le Roi de la Forêt

- une fable Chinoise

The King of the Forest

- a Chinese Fable

retold by Dawn Casey
illustrated by Jago

French translation by
Annie Arnold

Le Renard marchait dans la forêt quand il entendit quelque chose bouger dans l'herbe haute.

BRUISSEMENT Quelque chose de gros.
BATTEMENT Quelque chose avec des yeux jaunes.
JAILLISSEMENT Quelque chose avec des dents comme des couteaux.

Fox was walking in the forest when he heard something moving in the long grass.

RUSTLE Something big.
BLINK Something with yellow eyes.
FLASH Something with teeth like knives.

« Bonjour petit renard, » le Tigre sourit à belles dents, et sa bouche n'était que dents. Le Renard eut un serrement de gorge.
« Je suis content de te rencontrer, » ronronna le Tigre, « je commençais juste a avoir faim. »
Le Renard pensa rapidement. « Comment oses-tu ! » dit-il. « Ne sais-tu pas que je suis le Roi de la Forêt ? »
« Toi ! Roi de la Forêt ? » dit le Tigre, et il rit aux éclats.
« Si tu ne me crois pas, » répondit le Renard avec dignité, « marche derrière moi et tu verras – tout le monde a peur de moi. »
« Ça je dois le voir, » dit le Tigre.
Alors le Renard déambula dans la forêt. Le Tigre suivit derrière fièrement, avec sa queue tenue bien droite, jusqu'à…

"Good morning little fox," Tiger grinned, and his mouth was nothing but teeth. Fox gulped.
"I am pleased to meet you," Tiger purred. "I was just beginning to feel hungry."
Fox thought fast. "How dare you!" he said. "Don't you know I'm the King of the Forest?"
"You! King of the Forest?" said Tiger, and he roared with laughter.
"If you don't believe me," replied Fox with dignity, "walk behind me and you'll see – everyone is scared of me."
"This I've got to see," said Tiger.
So Fox strolled through the forest. Tiger followed behind proudly, with his tail held high, until…

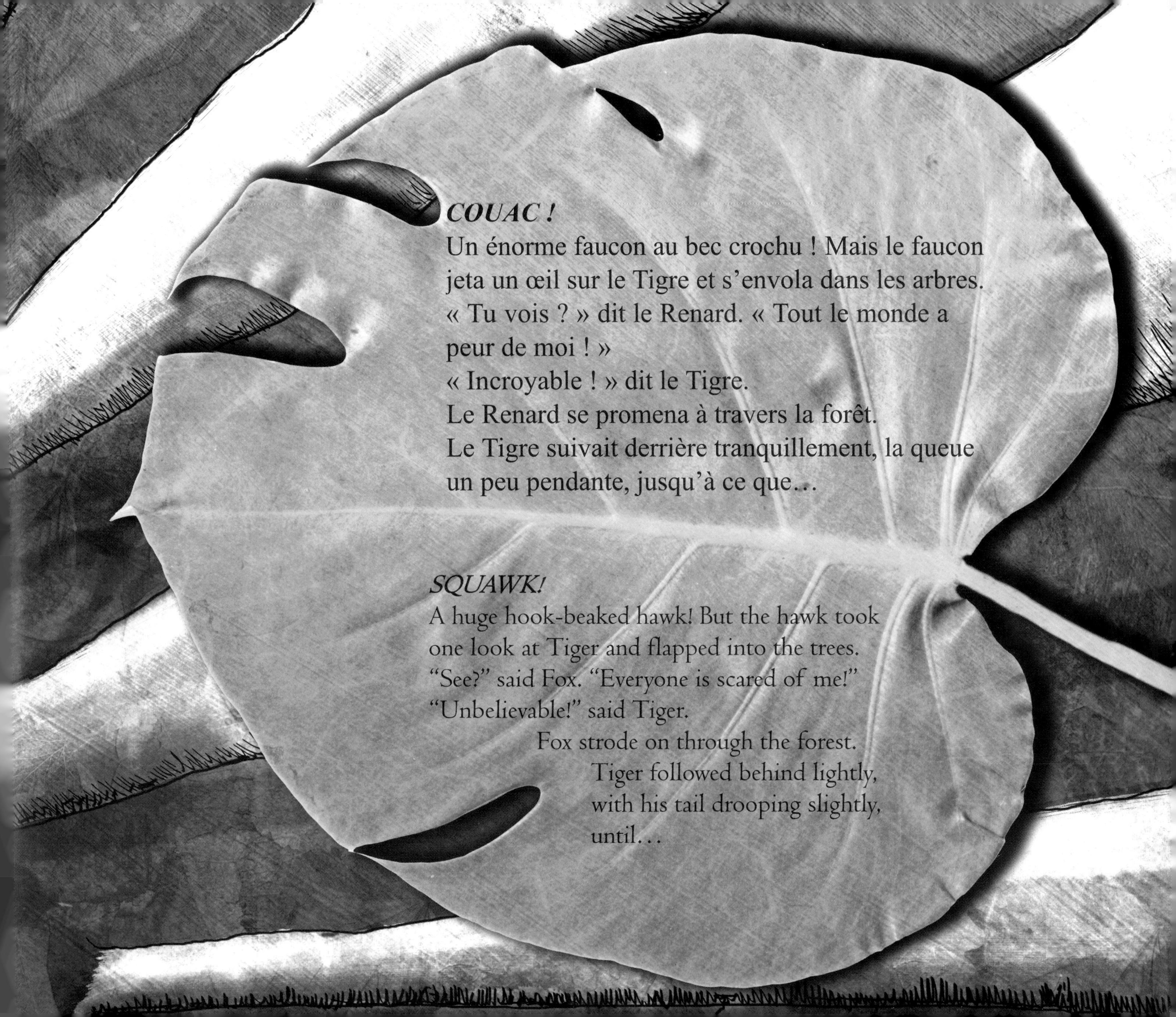

COUAC !
Un énorme faucon au bec crochu ! Mais le faucon jeta un œil sur le Tigre et s'envola dans les arbres.
« Tu vois ? » dit le Renard. « Tout le monde a peur de moi ! »
« Incroyable ! » dit le Tigre.
Le Renard se promena à travers la forêt.
Le Tigre suivait derrière tranquillement, la queue un peu pendante, jusqu'à ce que…

SQUAWK!
A huge hook-beaked hawk! But the hawk took one look at Tiger and flapped into the trees.
"See?" said Fox. "Everyone is scared of me!"
"Unbelievable!" said Tiger.
Fox strode on through the forest.
Tiger followed behind lightly,
with his tail drooping slightly,
until…

GRRR !

Un gros ours noir ! Mais l'ours jeta un coup d'œil au Tigre et s'enfonça dans les buissons.

« Tu vois ? » dit le Renard. « Tout le monde a peur de moi ! »

« Incroyable ! » dit le Tigre.

Le renard traversa la forêt. Le Tigre suivait derrière humblement, la queue traînant sur le sol de la forêt, jusqu'à ce que…

GROWL!

A big black bear! But the bear took one look at Tiger and crashed into the bushes.

"See?" said Fox. "Everyone is scared of me!"

"Incredible!" said Tiger.

Fox marched on through the forest. Tiger followed behind meekly, with his tail dragging on the forest floor, until…

SSSS !
Un serpent svelte et glissant ! Mais le serpent jeta un coup d'œil au Tigre et glissa dans les broussailles.
« TU VOIS ? » dit le Renard. « TOUT LE MONDE A PEUR DE MOI ! »

HISSSSSSS!
A slinky slidey snake! But the snake took one look at Tiger and slithered into the undergrowth.
"SEE?" said Fox. "EVERYONE IS SCARED OF ME!"

« Je vois, » dit le Tigre, « tu es le Roi de la Forêt et je suis ton humble serviteur. »
« Bien, » dit le Renard. « Alors, va-t-en ! »

Et le Tigre partit, la queue entre les jambes.

"I do see," said Tiger, "you are the King of the Forest and I am your humble servant."
"Good," said Fox. "Then, be gone!"

And Tiger went, with his tail between his legs.

« Le Roi de la Forêt, » se dit le Renard avec un sourire. Son sourire s'épanouit, et se transforma en rire nerveux, et le Renard rit très fort tout le chemin du retour.

"King of the Forest," said Fox to himself with a smile. His smile grew into a grin, and his grin grew into a giggle, and Fox laughed out loud all the way home.

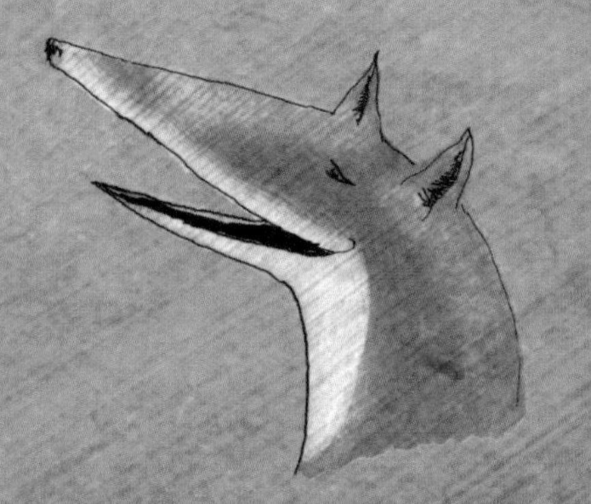

To my Nana, with love - DC

For my wife, Alex - J

First published in 2006 by Mantra Lingua Ltd
Global House, 303 Ballards Lane
London N12 8NP
www.mantralingua.com

A CIP record for this book is available from the British Library